For John
Manuela Olten

First American edition published in 2007
by Boxer Books Limited.

Distributed in the United States and Canada by
Sterling Publishing Co., Inc.
387 Park Avenue South, New York, NY 10016-8810

Published in Great Britain in 2007
by Boxer Books Limited.
www.boxerbooks.com

First published as *Echte Kerle* by Bajazzo Verlag, Zurich 2004.

Text and illustrations copyright © 2004 Manuela Olten

Original translated text copyright © 2007 Boxer Books Limited

ISBN 13: 978-1-905417-48-3
ISBN 10: 1-905417-48-9

3 5 7 9 10 8 6 4 2

Printed in China

BOYS
ARE BEST!

Manuela Olten

Boxer Books

Boys are best!

Girls are

And changing their dolls' clothes!

On and off

on

on

on

off

off

off

off

off   off

on   on

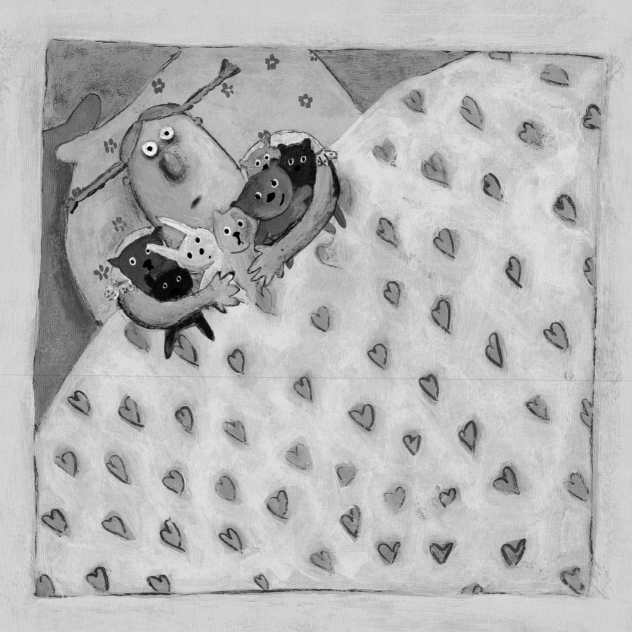

Girls take their silly teddy bears to bed with them every night.

Girls are such

scaredy
cats!

Yeah! When they're really scared,

they wet their **pants!**

Girls are even scared of

ghosts!

G-G-Ghosts?

Oh.

Boys are so silly!